HOW NOBURO BECA NINJA

Pari Kan

Illustrations by M. Naveed

Dedicated to my daughter Mimi

Noburo was a five-year-old boy who wanted to become a ninja when he grew up. But he was not confident that he could.

Noboru smiled. He loved her stories.

Then he missed his school bus.

He fell into a puddle.

When he got up, a dog was eating the sandwich from his lunchbox.

He was late to school.

He forgot everything he had studied for the big test.

His teacher wrote a letter to Thomas' parents, which seemed as long as ten trains to Thomas.

With tears in his eyes, Thomas returned from school and handed over the letter to his mom.

But his mom was not upset when she read the letter. She knew the great secret of life. She knelt in front of Thomas and said,

"What you choose to believe about yourself is what you will become."

Thomas felt doubtful. He didn't believe in himself.

But his mom praised him. "Your teacher writes that you are a genius. There's no need to cry, Thomas. You should be proud."

Thomas believed his mom.

He became confident in himself.

He believed he was a genius and realized that he was always full of good ideas.

One day he wanted to play outside, but it was raining. He immediately had an idea.

He sketched out a design and made a tent so that he could play outside and stay dry.

Another time, he wanted jam from the top shelf in the kitchen. He couldn't reach that high.

He had an idea.

He dreamt BIG. He even dreamt of landing on the moon one day.

And when he grew up, he became an astronaut and did visit the moon.

When Granny finished the story of Thomas, Noburo too had learnt the great secret of life.

And Noburo took the 'BIG' decision to become a ninja.

To be continued...........

Self-confidence tip from Ninja kid Noburo

Look into the mirror and say to yourself, 'I am confident. I am enough.'

Do it just after waking up, once in the daytime, and at night before going to bed.

Repeat at least for 21 days and see the MAGIC happen.

"Believe and your belief will create the fact."- William James

Review

Thank you so much for purchasing this book! I hope you had a great experience reading it to your child. If you enjoyed reading this book, I'd be grateful if you could take a moment to post a review on Amazon. I'd love to hear from you. Thank you for your time and support.

OTHER BOOKS

Printed in Great Britain
by Amazon